GREAT TALES FROM LONG AGO

BEOWULF AND THE MONSTERS

Retold by Margaret Berrill
Illustrated by Paul Crompton

Methuen Children's Books

in association with Belitha Press Ltd.

Note : The story of *Beowulf* first came to
Britain with Germanic invaders, but we know
it from the long poem written down hundreds
of years later, in about the year 1000. It is
written in the language now called Anglo-
Saxon or Old English from which our modern
English developed. The story told here is
from the first part of the poem. Some of the
events described elsewhere in the poem took
place in fifth- and sixth-century Scandinavia.
The Geats and the Danes were real tribes,
and we know where Heorot was. King
Hrothgar and King Hygelac existed, but no
evidence has been found to suggest that
there was ever a real man on whom the
superhuman figure of Beowulf was based.

The name of Hygelac is pronounced "Huge-
yer-lack" and Wealtheow is pronounced
"Whale-thou".

MB

Copyright © in this format Belitha Press Ltd, 1988
Text copyright © Margaret Berrill 1988
Illustrations copyright © Paul Crompton 1988
Art Director: Treld Bicknell
First published in Great Britain in 1988
by Methuen Children's Books Ltd,
11 New Fetter Lane, London EC4P 4EE
Conceived, designed and produced by Belitha Press Ltd,
31 Newington Green, London N16 9PU
ISBN 0 416 96230 0 (hardback)
Printed in Hong Kong by South China Printing Co.

ONCE, LONG AGO IN THE NORTHLANDS,
a famous king of the Danes called Hrothgar
built a great hall.
Its name was Heorot.
King Hrothgar held feasts in Heorot
and gave gold and treasure to his loyal followers
who had fought bravely beside him in many battles.
Firelight flickered on the walls
and the rafters rang with music and laughter
as the warriors feasted.
Minstrels played their harps and told stories
of the great deeds of heroes long since dead.

B**UT OUTSIDE IN THE DARKNESS**
was a terrible monster called Grendel
who roamed the moors and marshes.
Grendel could not bear the sounds of happiness
that came from Heorot.
When the warriors had settled down to sleep
he came to Heorot and burst into the hall.
From his wrist hung a huge glove made of dragon skins.
He snatched up thirty warriors as they lay sleeping
and carried them off in his glove
over the misty moors
to his home in the lake of the water demons.

AT DAYBREAK, WHEN THEY SAW WHAT GRENDEL HAD DONE, the Danes were filled with grief and rage. King Hrothgar especially mourned his dead followers. Night after night Grendel returned.

He killed and carried off more warriors.

And so it went on for twelve years

until the great hall was always left empty after nightfall.

The warriors who remained alive

were afraid to sleep in Heorot.

Instead they made beds for themselves

in the other buildings.

If any warrior dared spend the night in Heorot

he would have disappeared by morning.

THEN THROUGHOUT THE NORTHLANDS,
minstrels told the tale
of Grendel's war against Hrothgar.
In his own land, Beowulf,
a brave warrior of Hygelac, king of the Geats,
heard the sad story.

King Hygelac, who was Beowulf's uncle,
begged him not to go,
but Beowulf was determined to cross the sea
to help the old king of the Danes.
He chose fourteen of the bravest warriors
and they sailed for two days.
Then they saw cliffs and mountains ahead.
The warriors went ashore and tied up their ship.

As SOON AS THEY HAD LANDED,
the Danish coastguard came galloping along the shore
shaking his spear at them.
He could tell by their shields and armour
that they had not come in peace.

Beowulf told him that they wanted
to help the Danes in the war against Grendel.
The coastguard agreed to take them to Heorot.

THE GEATS PILED UP THEIR SHIELDS AND SPEARS
outside the great hall,
and, wearing their helmets and armour,
went in to greet King Hrothgar.
Beowulf told him about the brave deeds
he had done in the past against giants and monsters.
"Do not refuse my request, King Hrothgar," said Beowulf
"I want to drive Grendel out of Heorot on my own
with only the help of my noble warriors.
Grendel does not use any weapons
so I will tackle him with my bare hands."

Hrothgar welcomed the Geats to Heorot.
He thanked Beowulf and agreed to his request.
A bench was cleared for Beowulf and his men.
Minstrels made music
and the Danes and Geats enjoyed a feast together.
Queen Wealtheow gave Beowulf mead in a jewelled cup
and thanked him for coming to help the Danes.
"Tomorrow," said Beowulf,
"you will be able to drink your mead without fear
in Heorot."

AT NIGHTFALL THE DANES LEFT THE HALL
while the Geats stayed to keep watch.
Beowulf took off his armour
and gave his sword to a servant, true to his word
that he would face Grendel without weapons.

Then the Geats lay down to sleep.
Each one was thinking
that he might never see his home again.
At dead of night Grendel came stalking over the misty moors.
He tore the great doors from their hinges and burst into the hall.

Grendel snatched up one of the sleeping warriors
and greedily ate him. Next he came to Beowulf
and tried to seize and eat him.
But Beowulf leapt up, ready to fight.
He grasped Grendel with his bare hands
and a mighty struggle began.
Heorot echoed with the din
as benches and gold cups crashed to the floor.
The Geats snatched up their swords
hoping to help Beowulf in the fight.
They did not know that Grendel had magic powers
so that no weapon could hurt him.
Beowulf held Grendel's right hand in his fierce grip.
Grendel wrenched himself away, shrieking with pain,
for his right arm had been torn off.
He staggered out of the hall and made off to his home
in the lake of the water demons.

GRENDEL HAD RECEIVED A DEADLY WOUND.
When daybreak came, there in the hall for all to see
hung the huge arm and clawed hand
which Beowulf had torn from the monster's body.
That night a great feast was held in Heorot
and Hrothgar gave Beowulf and the Geats
treasures of gold, jewels, horses and armour.
The old king gave the young warrior
his own jewelled saddle which he had used in many battles.
"I cannot reward you highly enough," said Hrothgar,
"but you have won the greatest prize on earth,
because now you will be famous forever
and people will remember your name
long after you are dead."

AFTER THE FEAST THE KING AND QUEEN
and Beowulf left the hall.
A large group of warriors settled down to sleep,
each one with his weapons and armour at his head.
One of them would never wake again.
From her home on the misty moors
Grendel's mother was coming
to take revenge for the death of her son.
In the darkness she burst into Heorot,
snatched up one of the Danes and carried him off to her lair.
She took Grendel's hand and arm with her.
None of the warriors could prevent her from escaping.

As soon as he heard the terrible news next morning King Hrothgar called for Beowulf.
"Some people say that they have seen two monsters on the moors," he said.
"One was Grendel, and the other had the shape of a woman.
Would you dare to follow this monster
to her dreadful lair?"
Beowulf replied that, once again,
he would try to make his name famous,
even if he should die in the battle.

Hrothgar, Beowulf and their warriors set out to follow the footprints of Grendel's mother.
At last they came to the deep lake
where Grendel and his mother lived.
Dragons and other monsters lay upon the cliffs
or swam in the deep water.
They scuttled off when the warriors blew their war horns.
Beowulf put on his armour and, taking his sword,
dived into the lake.

Nearly a day went by before he reached the bottom.
Grendel's mother was waiting for him.
She grabbed him with her terrible claws
and swarms of sea creatures attacked him.
His armour saved him from wounds
but Grendel's mother carried him away to her huge cave
where Grendel's body lay.
Beowulf broke free and swung at the monster with his sword
but it could not wound her. A fierce struggle began
and each in turn flung the other to the floor.
Suddenly Beowulf noticed a huge sword
hanging on the wall. It had been made by giants
and was too big for most men to handle.
With a mighty effort, he swung it at Grendel's mother
and killed her.

THE WARRIORS HAD BEEN WAITING FOR HOURS BESIDE THE LAKE.
When they saw the water all churned up
and stained with blood,
King Hrothgar and the Danes thought that Beowulf was dead.
Sadly they turned for home.
But the Geats stayed on, hoping against hope
to see their friend and leader again.
They were not disappointed, for at last Beowulf swam ashore.
He had left Grendel's mother lying dead in her cave,
but he carried with him Grendel's head
and the jewelled sword hilt.
The blade had been melted by the monster's blood.
Four of the Geats carried Grendel's head on a spear.
They went in triumph to Heorot
to tell King Hrothgar and Queen Wealtheow
what Beowulf had done.

NEXT DAY THE GEATS WERE LONGING TO GO HOME.
Hrothgar gave Beowulf twelve gifts
and tears streamed down the old king's face.
He was thinking that he might never see Beowulf again.
Beowulf promised to return
if Hrothgar should ever need his help.
The Geats went back to their ship
and loaded the horses and treasure on board.

This time the coastguard gave them a warm welcome. Beowulf gave him a sword decorated with gold.

WHEN THEY REACHED GEATLAND,
Beowulf and his men walked in the sunshine
to King Hygelac's hall.
They were welcomed there as heroes.
Beowulf handed over to King Hygelac
the treasure which Hrothgar had given him.
In return, Hygelac gave the brave warrior
a hall, great lands and treasure.
From now on Beowulf would be a chieftain of the Geats.
One day he would be their king,
and rule them well for fifty years.
And for years to come throughout the northlands,
when warriors gathered in their great halls,
minstrels would tell the tale of Beowulf and the monsters.

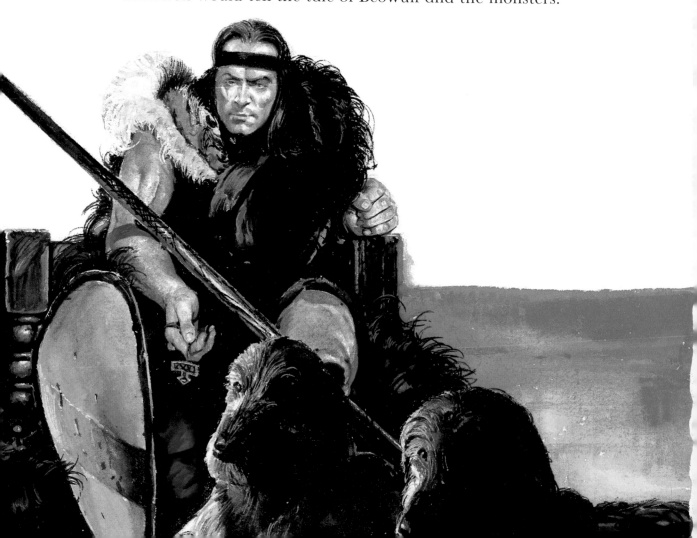